Mark Twain's
Adventures of Tom Sawyer

Tom Sawyer
Becomes a Pirate

Adapted by I.M. Richardson
Illustrated by Bert Dodson

Troll Associates

Library of Congress Cataloging in Publication Data

Richardson, I. M.
    Tom Sawyer becomes a pirate.

    (Adventures of Tom Sawyer; 2)
    Summary: Tom, Huck, and Joe Harper appear at their
own ''funeral;'' Tom has problems with Becky; and an
innocent man goes on trial for a murder Injun Joe
committed.
    [1. Missouri—Fiction]   I. Dodson, Bert, ill.
II. Twain, Mark, 1835-1910. Adventures of Tom Sawyer.
III. Title.   IV. Series: Richardson, I. M. Adventures
of Tom Sawyer.
PZ7.R3948Toe 1984   [Fic]   83-18037
ISBN 0-8167-0061-3 (lib. bdg.)
ISBN 0-8167-0062-1 (pbk.)

10 9 8 7 6 5 4 3 2

When Tom Sawyer awoke, he wondered where he was. Then he remembered. He was on Jackson's Island. He and Joe Harper and Huckleberry Finn had run away and become pirates. They had landed their raft on the small island about two o'clock that morning, built a fire, and fried up some bacon. Finally they had fallen asleep.

Tom woke Huck and Joe, and they raced down to the water for a swim. After breakfast they explored the island, and after lunch they sat around and talked. Then the talk died, and they started to get bored. Soon they grew homesick, but no one would admit it. As they sat there, they heard a deep, booming sound in the distance.

4

"What's that?" asked Joe. "Somebody's drowned!" Tom exclaimed. "That's it!" agreed Huck. "They shoot a cannon over the water, and that makes the body come up to the top. I'd give heaps to know who it is." Suddenly Tom cried, "Say, I know who's drowned—it's *us!* They think we drowned in the river, and they're searching for our bodies." They were famous! It was worthwhile being pirates after all.

When the cannon had stopped firing, the boys caught some
fish, cooked supper, and sat around the fire. Now that the
excitement was over, Joe and Tom felt homesick again.
That night Tom left a note in Joe's hat and stole off into the
dark. Before midnight, he was peeking through the window
of his aunt's sitting room. He saw Aunt Polly, Mrs. Harper,
his younger brother Sid, and his cousin Mary.

Tom sneaked to the door and slowly pushed on it. When it
was open wide enough, he crawled through and disappeared
under the bed. A breeze blew through the open door, and
Sid got up to close it. Aunt Polly and Mrs. Harper were
crying and talking about the boys. "If their bodies aren't
found by Sunday," sobbed Aunt Polly, "the funeral
services will be held without them."

When Aunt Polly was alone and sound asleep, Tom crept out from under the bed and placed a note on the table. Suddenly he had an idea. He put the note back into his pocket, kissed his sleeping aunt, and sneaked out as quietly as he had come in. Before long, he was rowing back across the river in a "borrowed" boat.

The night was nearly over when he reached Jackson's Island. By the time he got back to camp, it was daylight. Huck and Joe were already awake. As they ate breakfast, Tom told them all about his adventure. Then, while the others went fishing and exploring, Tom hid himself in a shady nook and slept until noon.

For the next two days, the boys hunted for turtle eggs, swam in the river, and rolled in the sand. They played circus and marbles until they grew tired and bored and homesick. Tom missed Becky Thatcher. He caught himself writing "Becky" in the sand with his big toe and quickly erased it. But he could not keep from writing it again. Finally Joe said, "It's so *lonesome*. I want to go home."

"You'll feel better by and by," said Tom. But Joe would not change his mind. He started to walk away, and Huck got up and went off with him. Tom suddenly noticed how quiet it had become. He knew that only his secret plan could stop his friends from leaving. "Wait!" he cried. "I have an idea." When he told them his plan, they shouted for joy and agreed to stay.

That night, Joe and Tom smoked a pipe for the first time and got very sick. Around midnight, streaks of lightning turned night into day, and heavy rains pounded the island. The boys huddled in a tent under a sycamore tree. Then, when the wind blew the tent away, they were forced to find better shelter. When morning came, they realized how lucky they were. Lightning had struck the very spot where their tent had been!

The new day dragged slowly on, and the boys began to feel homesick again. Tom reminded them of their plan, and that raised their spirits. They spent the rest of the day playing Indians. They painted their bodies with "war paint" and raced off to attack a settlement. That night, they smoked their pipes without getting quite as sick as they had before.

On Sunday morning, the villagers gathered at the church for the boys' funeral services. No one could remember when the church had been so full. Tom's and Joe's families came dressed in black and sat in the front row. The preacher spoke so warmly about the dear departed boys that everyone was moved to tears.

Suddenly there was a sound in the choir loft. The preacher raised his tear-filled eyes and stared in disbelief. One after another, people turned to see what the preacher was looking at. Then everyone rose and stared as the three "dead" boys came marching down the aisle! That had been Tom's secret plan—to hide in the choir loft and attend their own funeral. Aunt Polly turned white. She was both mad and glad—but mostly glad!

The next morning, Tom decided to play a trick on his aunt. "Last Wednesday night I dreamed about you, Aunt Polly," he said. "You and Mrs. Harper were here, and you were both crying. The wind blew the door open, and Sid closed it." His aunt was amazed. "Why, that's right!" she exclaimed. "It happened just that way! Go on, Tom, tell me more." As soon as Tom had finished, Aunt Polly ran off to tell Mrs. Harper about the marvelous "dream."

At school, Tom and Joe were heroes. Smaller boys followed them around the schoolyard. Boys their own age were filled with envy. The former pirates felt as if they had reached their highest glory. Tom decided that fame and glory were enough for him. He did not need Becky Thatcher anymore.

Tom ignored Becky and talked with Amy Lawrence instead. Becky hid her anger and pretended to be happy. Suddenly she saw Mary Austin and called out, "I'm going to have a picnic, Mary! Can you come?" At once, everyone begged for invitations—except Tom. Tears came to Becky's eyes, and she promised herself she would get even with him.

At recess, Tom thought he would get Becky jealous again, but Becky had a plan of her own. When Tom saw her, a chill shot through his heart. She was out behind the school building, looking at a picture book. And next to her was that rich smarty-pants, Alfred Temple! Tom stole out of the schoolyard and went home feeling lower than ever before.

As soon as Becky saw that Tom had left, she burst into tears. Alfred tried to comfort her, but she cried, "Leave me alone! I hate you." Then Alfred knew that she had used him to get back at Tom. So he went into the empty schoolhouse and poured ink all over Tom's spelling book. Becky saw him do it, and she knew Tom would be whipped for it.

As soon as Tom got home, Aunt Polly said, "I ought to skin you alive! There I was, telling Joe Harper's mother all that rubbish about your 'dream.' And then she says Joe told her *you came home Wednesday night!* You saw it all, first-hand! How could you let me go and make a fool of myself like that?" Tom felt bad. "I guess I didn't think," he said.

Then Tom told his aunt why he had sneaked home that
night. "I wrote a note that said: *We ain't dead—we are only
off being pirates.* And I left it for you," said Tom. "But
then I didn't want to spoil the joke about the funeral, so I
put the note back into my pocket." Later, when Aunt Polly
found the note in Tom's jacket pocket, tears of love poured
from her eyes.

22

On the way back to school, Tom saw Becky. "I acted mean today, and I'm sorry," he said. "Let's make up, okay?" Becky just stuck her nose up and said, "I'll thank you to leave me alone, Thomas Sawyer. I'll never speak to you again." Then she marched off and disappeared inside the schoolhouse. Tom was too shocked to snap back with something witty, like "Who cares, Miss Smarty!"

In the schoolmaster's desk was a mysterious book that every student was curious about. As Becky passed, she noticed that the desk drawer was open. The room was empty, so she opened the book to take a peek. Just then, Tom came in. Becky was so startled that she ripped a page in the school-master's book! She quickly shoved the book back into the drawer and fled from the room.

That afternoon, Tom was whipped for spilling ink on his spelling book. Becky was glad, because she was sure Tom was going to tell on her for what she had done. A few minutes later, the schoolmaster opened his mysterious book and cried out, "Who did this?" No one spoke. He asked each of the students and watched their faces for some sign of guilt. "Joseph Harper? Benjamin Rogers? Amy Lawrence?" Becky was next.

The schoolmaster said, "Rebecca Thatcher, did you tear this book?" A thought shot like lightning through Tom's brain. He sprang to his feet and shouted, "*I* done it!" Everyone stared at Tom's incredible folly. But as he stepped up to take the punishment, Tom saw surprise, gratitude, and adoration shining in Becky's eyes. And that was worth a hundred whippings!

On examination day, the boys and girls had to stand up and recite their final lessons in front of their parents and classmates. Suddenly someone lowered a cat through a trap door in the ceiling. The cat grabbed the schoolmaster's wig and was quickly pulled back up to the attic. Everyone laughed so hard that class was dismissed. Vacation had come!

In the middle of the summer, Muff Potter's murder trial began. Injun Joe said that Potter had gotten drunk and killed a man in the graveyard. Tom and Huck knew that was a lie, because they had seen Injun Joe commit the murder himself! The boys were too scared to tell anyone what they had seen. So even though they felt sorry for poor old Muff Potter, they had agreed to keep quiet.

28

As the trial continued, Tom's conscience bothered him more and more. He wanted to help Muff Potter, but he was too scared. So he just hung around outside the courtroom, listening for hopeful news. None came. The evidence was piling up against Potter, and no one knew Injun Joe was lying. Tom's conscience grew unbearable. That night, he finally did something about it.

The next day, the courthouse was packed. One witness said he saw Potter washing in a brook on the night of the murder. Another witness said Potter's knife was found near the corpse. Potter's lawyer did not cross-examine even one of the witnesses. When the prosecutor finally said, "We rest our case," everyone figured Muff Potter was done for.

Suddenly the defense lawyer stood up and said, "Call Thomas Sawyer to the stand!" There was a buzz of excitement as Tom was sworn in. Then everyone listened as he told about that awful night. As his terrible tale reached its climax, Tom said, "Muff Potter was knocked out. Then Injun Joe grabbed Potter's knife and stabbed . . . " *Crash!* Quick as lightning, Injun Joe jumped through the window and ran for his life.

Injun Joe escaped, but Muff Potter's life was saved. Tom became a hero once more. The grownups were proud of him, and every youngster in town envied him. His name appeared in the village paper. And some people even believed he might one day be president—if only he could stay out of trouble long enough!